MR. NOSEY

by Roger Hargreaves

Mr Nosey liked to know about everything that was going on.

He was always poking his nose into other people's business.

Mr Nosey was the sort of a person who, if they came upon a locked door, couldn't resist looking through the keyhole to see why the door had been locked.

Mr Nosey was the sort of a person who, if he found an unopened letter addressed to somebody else, would simply have to open it to find out what was inside.

Mrr Brown,
16 High Street,
Tiddletown

Mr Nosey was the sort of a person who, if he was sitting reading his paper on a train, would much rather read the paper of the person sitting next to him.

Naturally, as you might well imagine, Mr Nosey was not very popular.

People did not like the way in which Mr Nosey would peek and pry into their affairs.

They did not like it at all, but did that stop Mr Nosey peeking and prying?

It did not!

Mr Nosey lived in a funny tall thin house in a place called Tiddletown.

The people of Tiddletown decided that Mr Nosey was becoming much too nosey, and so they held a meeting to discuss what to do about him.

"We must find some way of stopping him being so nosey," said old Mr Chips the town carpenter.

"That's right!" said Mrs Washer who ran the Tiddletown laundry. "He needs to be taught a lesson."

"If only we could think of a way to stop him poking his nose into everything," said Mr Brush the painter.

And then, a small smile spread over his face.

"Listen," he said, now grinning. "I have a plan!"

All his friends gathered round to listen to his plan.

The following morning Mr Nosey was out walking along Tiddletown High Street when he heard somebody whistling behind one of the closed doors.

"I wonder what's going on here?" he thought to himself, and tiptoeing up to the door he quietly opened it and peeped in.

"SPLASH" went a very wet paint brush right on the end of Mr Nosey's nose covering it with bright red paint.

"Oh dear. I AM sorry!" said Mr Brush, who was painting the inside of the door.

Poor Mr Nosey had to go straight home to try and remove the red paint, which was very difficult and rather painful.

Mr Brush chuckled to himself.

The Plan had begun.

The following day Mr Nosey was walking past the laundry when he heard somebody laughing on the other side of the wall.

"I wonder what's going on here?" he thought to himself, and standing on tiptoe he looked over the wall.

"SNAP" went a clothes peg right on the end of Mr Nosey's nose.

"Oh dear. I AM sorry!" said Mrs Washer, who was hanging up clothes on a washing line on the other side of the wall.

Poor Mr Nosey removed the clothes peg, and went off down the street feeling extremely sorry for himself and for his poor red nose.

Mrs Washer chuckled to herself.

The Plan was working.

The next day Mr Nosey was going past a fence when he heard hammering.

"I wonder what's going on here?" he thought to himself, and creeping very quietly to the end of the fence he peeped round.

"BANG" went a hammer right on the end of
Mr Nosey's nose.

"Oh dear. I AM sorry!" said old Mr Chips, who was
nailing up a loose plank in the fence.

Poor Mr Nosey had to go home immediately and
bandage his poor red sore nose.

Mr Chips grinned a broad grin.

The Plan was working very well indeed.

The following day Mr Nosey was walking in the woods when he heard somebody sawing wood.

"I wonder what's going on here?" he thought to himself, and he crept up behind a tree.

He was just about to peer out from behind the tree when it suddenly occurred to him that if he did, something very nasty might happen to his nose.

And so, he went on his way without being nosey.

Behind the tree, with a saw raised in his hand, stood Mr Herd the farmer.

When he saw that Mr Nosey had gone on his way without being nosey he laughed and laughed and laughed.

The Plan had worked.

Mr Herd hurried into Tiddletown to tell everybody.

The Plan really had worked because after that Mr Nosey stopped being nosey and soon became very good friends with everybody in Tiddletown.

And that is the end of the story, except to say that if you are ever tempted to be as nosey as Mr Nosey used to be you'd better expect one thing.

A sore nose!

3 Great Offers for MR.MEN Fans!

1 New Mr. Men or Little Miss Library Bus Presentation Cases

A brand new stronger, roomier school bus
library box, with sturdy carrying handle
and stay-closed fasteners.
The full colour, wipe-clean boxes make
a great home for your full collection.
They're just £5.99 inc P&P and free bookmark!

☐ MR. MEN   ☐ LITTLE MISS (please tick and order overleaf)

2 Door Hangers and Posters

In every Mr. Men and Little Miss book
like this one, you will find a special
token. Collect 6 tokens and we will
send you a brilliant Mr. Men or Little
Miss poster and a Mr. Men or Little
Miss double sided full colour
bedroom door hanger of your
choice. Simply tick your choice in the
list and tape a 50p coin for your
two items to this page.

PLEASE STICK YOUR 50P COIN HERE

Door Hangers (please tick)
☐ Mr. Nosey & Mr. Muddle
☐ Mr. Slow & Mr. Busy
☐ Mr. Messy & Mr. Quiet
☐ Mr. Perfect & Mr. Forgetful
☐ Little Miss Fun & Little Miss Late
☐ Little Miss Helpful & Little Miss Tidy
☐ Little Miss Busy & Little Miss Brainy
☐ Little Miss Star & Little Miss Fun

Posters (please tick)
☐ MR.MEN
☐ LITTLE MISS

3 Sixteen Beautiful Fridge Magnets – any 2 for £2.00! inc.P&P

They're very special collector's items!
Simply tick your first and second* choices from the list below
of any 2 characters!

1st Choice
- [ ] Mr. Happy
- [ ] Mr. Lazy
- [ ] Mr. Topsy-Turvy
- [ ] Mr. Bounce
- [ ] Mr. Bump
- [ ] Mr. Small
- [ ] Mr. Snow
- [ ] Mr. Wrong

- [ ] Mr. Daydream
- [ ] Mr. Tickle
- [ ] Mr. Greedy
- [ ] Mr. Funny
- [ ] Little Miss Giggles
- [ ] Little Miss Splendid
- [ ] Little Miss Naughty
- [ ] Little Miss Sunshine

2nd Choice
- [ ] Mr. Happy
- [ ] Mr. Lazy
- [ ] Mr. Topsy-Turvy
- [ ] Mr. Bounce
- [ ] Mr. Bump
- [ ] Mr. Small
- [ ] Mr. Snow
- [ ] Mr. Wrong

- [ ] Mr. Daydream
- [ ] Mr. Tickle
- [ ] Mr. Greedy
- [ ] Mr. Funny
- [ ] Little Miss Giggles
- [ ] Little Miss Splendid
- [ ] Little Miss Naughty
- [ ] Little Miss Sunshine

*Only in case your first choice is out of stock.

---TO BE COMPLETED BY AN ADULT---

**To apply for any of these great offers, ask an adult to complete the coupon below and send it with
the appropriate payment and tokens, if needed, to MR. MEN CLASSIC OFFER, PO BOX 715, HORSHAM RH12 5WG**

- [ ] Please send ____ Mr. Men Library case(s) and/or ____ Little Miss Library case(s) at £5.99 each inc P&P
- [ ] Please send a poster and door hanger as selected overleaf. I enclose six tokens plus a 50p coin for P&P
- [ ] Please send me ____ pair(s) of Mr. Men/Little Miss fridge magnets, as selected above at £2.00 inc P&P

Fan's Name _____

Address _____

_____ **Postcode** _____

Date of Birth _____

Name of Parent/Guardian _____

Total amount enclosed £ _____

- [ ] **I enclose a cheque/postal order payable to Egmont Books Limited**
- [ ] **Please charge my MasterCard/Visa/Amex/Switch or Delta account** (delete as appropriate)

Card Number

Expiry date ___/___ **Signature** _____

Please allow 28 days for delivery. Offer is only available while stocks last. We reserve the right to change the terms
of this offer at any time and we offer a 14 day money back guarantee. This does not affect your statutory rights.
Data Protection Act: If you do not wish to receive other similar offers from us or companies we recommend, please
tick this box [ ]. Offers apply to UK only.

MR.MEN   LITTLE MISS
Mr. Men and Little Miss™ & ©Mrs. Roger Hargreaves

CUT ALONG DOTTED LINE AND RETURN THIS WHOLE PAGE